THE Littlest NIGHT BEFORE CHRISTMAS

ILLUSTRATED BY MARY ENGELBREIT

Quill Tree Books
An Imprint of HarperCollinsPublishers

Library of Congress Control Number: 2022935083

ISBN 978-0-06-296933-0

22 23 24 25 26   RTLO   10 9 8 7 6 5 4 3 2 1
❖
First Edition

For my darling
Littlest
girls,
LOLA & ROXY

'Twas the night before Christmas

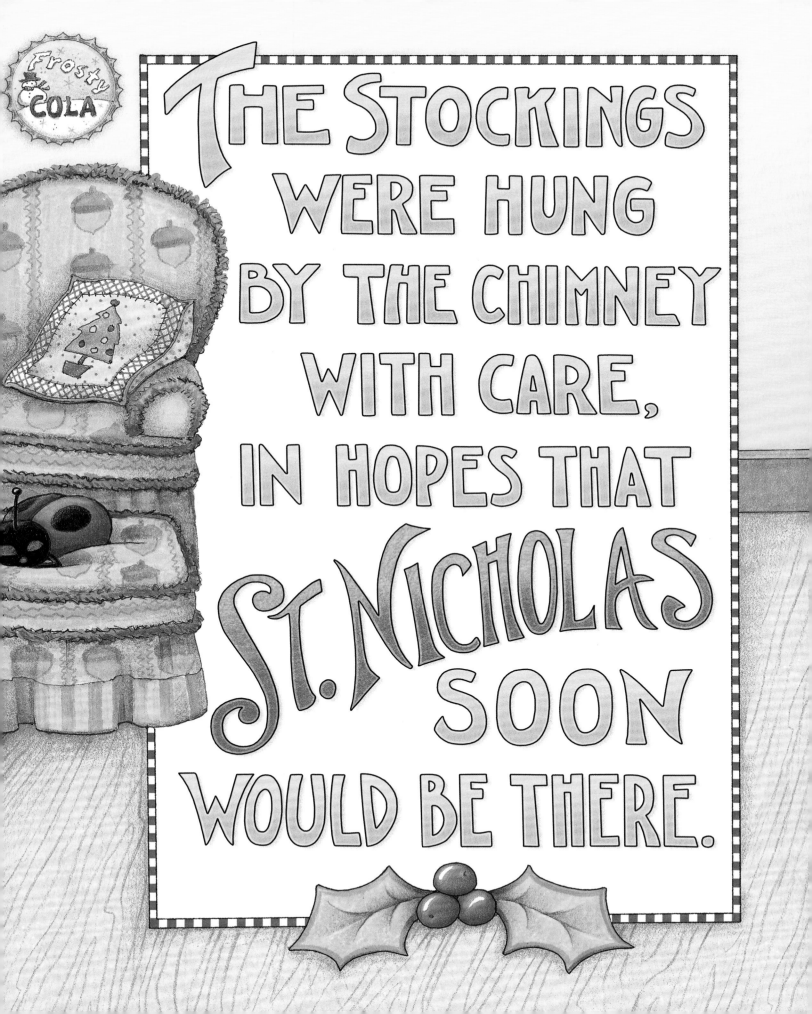

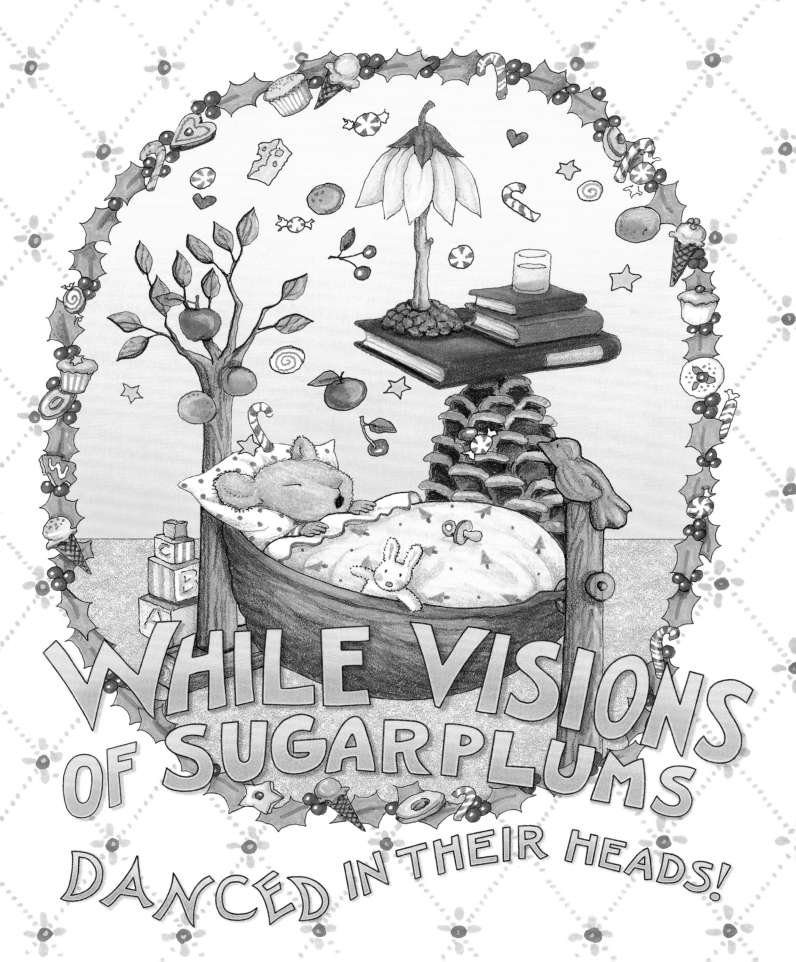

WHILE VISIONS OF SUGARPLUMS DANCED IN THEIR HEADS!

AND MAMA IN HER KERCHIEF,
AND I IN MY CAP,
HAD JUST SETTLED DOWN
FOR A LONG WINTER'S NAP...
WHEN OUT ON THE LAWN
THERE AROSE SUCH A
CLATTER,

I SPRANG FROM MY BED TO
SEE WHAT WAS THE MATTER.

THE MOON ON THE BREAST OF THE NEW-FALLEN SNOW GAVE A LUSTER OF MIDDAY TO OBJECTS BELOW.

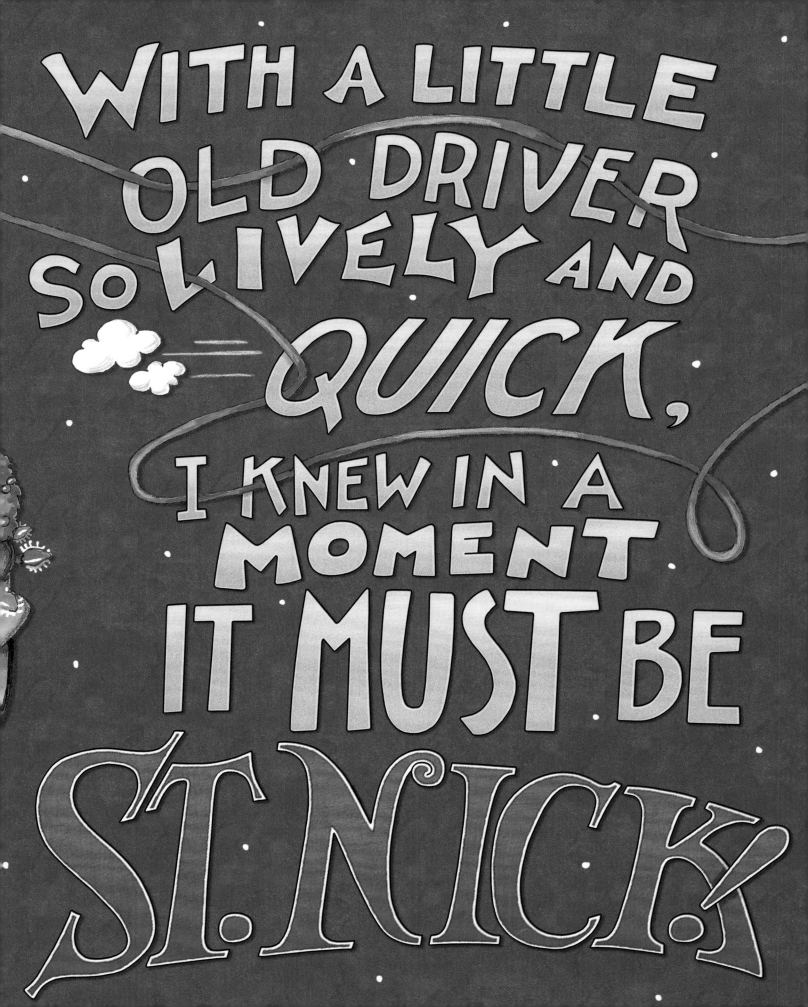

NOW DASHER! NOW DANCER!
NOW PRANCER AND VIXEN!
ON, COMET! ON, CUPID!

ON, DONDER AND BLITZEN!

To the TOP of the PORCH!
To the TOP of the WALL!
NOW DASH AWAY!
DASH AWAY!
DASH AWAY ALL!

AND THEN IN A ☆TWINKLING☆
ON THE ROOF I HEARD
THE PRANCING & PAWING OF EACH
LITTLE BIRD.

AS I DREW IN MY HEAD
AND WAS TURNING AROUND,
DOWN THE CHIMNEY
ST·NICHOLAS
Came with a BOUND!

A BUNDLE OF TOYS WAS FLUNG ON HIS BACK. AND HE LOOKED LIKE A PEDDLER JUST OPENING HIS PACK.

HIS EYES, HOW THEY TWINKLED!
HIS DIMPLES~HOW MERRY!
HIS CHEEKS WERE LIKE ROSES,
HIS NOSE LIKE A CHERRY!!

HIS DROLL LITTLE

MOUTH WAS DRAWN UP

LIKE A BOW

AND

THE BEARD

ON HIS CHIN

WAS AS

White

AS THE

SNOW.

A STICK OF PEPPERMINT HE HELD TIGHT IN HIS TEETH, AND HOLLY LEAVES ENCIRCLED HIS HEAD LIKE A WREATH.

HE HAD A BROAD FACE AND A LITTLE ROUND BELLY THAT SHOOK WHEN HE LAUGHED, LIKE A BOWLFUL OF JELLY!

HE SPRANG TO HIS SLEIGH,
TO HIS TEAM GAVE
A WHISTLE,
And away they all flew
LIKE THE
DOWN ON
A THISTLE.

BUT I HEARD HIM EXCLAIM

AS HE DROVE OUT OF SIGHT